BASEBALL, FOOTBALL, DADDY AND ME

By David Friend
Pictures by Rick Brown

PUFFIN BOOKS

PUFFIN BOOKS
Published by the Penguin Group
Viking Penguin, a division of Penguin Books USA Inc.,
375 Hudson Street, New York, New York 10014, U.S.A.
Penguin Books Ltd, 27 Wrights Lane, London W8 5TZ, England
Penguin Books Australia Ltd, Ringwood, Victoria, Australia
Penguin Books Canada Ltd, 10 Alcorn Avenue, Toronto, Ontario, Canada M4V 3B2
Penguin Books (N.Z.) Ltd, 182–190 Wairau Road, Auckland 10, New Zealand

Penguin Books Ltd, Registered Offices: Harmondsworth, Middlesex, England

First published in the United States of America by Viking Penguin,
a division of Penguin Books USA Inc., 1990
Published in Puffin Books, 1992
3   5   7   9   10   8   6   4
Text copyright © David Friend, 1990
Illustrations copyright © Rick Brown, 1990
LIBRARY OF CONGRESS CATALOGING-IN-PUBLICATION DATA
Friend, David, 1955–
Baseball, football, Daddy, and me / by David Friend ; illustrated
by Rick Brown.   p.   cm.
Summary: A little boy and his father enjoy a full assortment of
sporting events together.
ISBN 0-14-050914-3 (pbk.)
[1. Sports—Fiction.   2. Fathers and sons—Fiction.]   I. Brown,
Rick, 1946–   ill.   II. Title.
PZ7.F91525Bas   1992   [E]—dc20   91-30901

Printed in Japan
Set in Clarendon

For my father, Marty
Chicago's ultimate sports fan.
D.M.F.

For Ryan
R.B.

When Daddy takes me to the park
to watch a baseball game,

we cheer through popcorn boxes
as we shout the players' names.

When Daddy takes me to the field
to watch a football game,

we take hot soup and scarves and gloves
to fight the snow and rain.

When Daddy takes me to the court
to follow basketball,
I look up at the sky-high hoop
and wish I weren't so small.

When Daddy takes me to the track
to watch the horses race,

I see that jockeys aren't so tall
and feel less out-of-place.

When Daddy takes me to the course
to watch the golfers swing,
I'm not allowed to make a peep
—not even whispering.

When Daddy takes me to the rink
to watch hockey on ice,

I love to see the net goal light
that blinks red once or twice.

When Daddy takes me to the field
to watch a soccer match,

the players have to use their feet—
but goalies, they can catch.

When Daddy takes me to the court
to watch the tennis pros,

my neck hurts 'cause I watch the ball
bounce everywhere it goes.

You see, my daddy often likes
to put me on his lap.
He buttons my whole sweater up
and scrunches down my cap....

...He says stuff real loud about
a big, old tourny-ment,

then takes me to the stadium
to some big sports event.

Sometimes it's baseball,
sometimes football,
soccer, or hockey.
Whichever game he takes me to,
it's all the same to me....
Because I feel so lucky there
with all the other fans,
just sitting with my baseball cap
next to him in the stands.

But there's one favorite sport

that makes me happy as can be

when Daddy takes me to the park

to play catch—

JUST WITH ME!